HOME FRONT

CARELESS TALK

by Jack Wood

Illustrations by Tim Sell

FRANKLIN WATTS
LONDON • SYDNEY

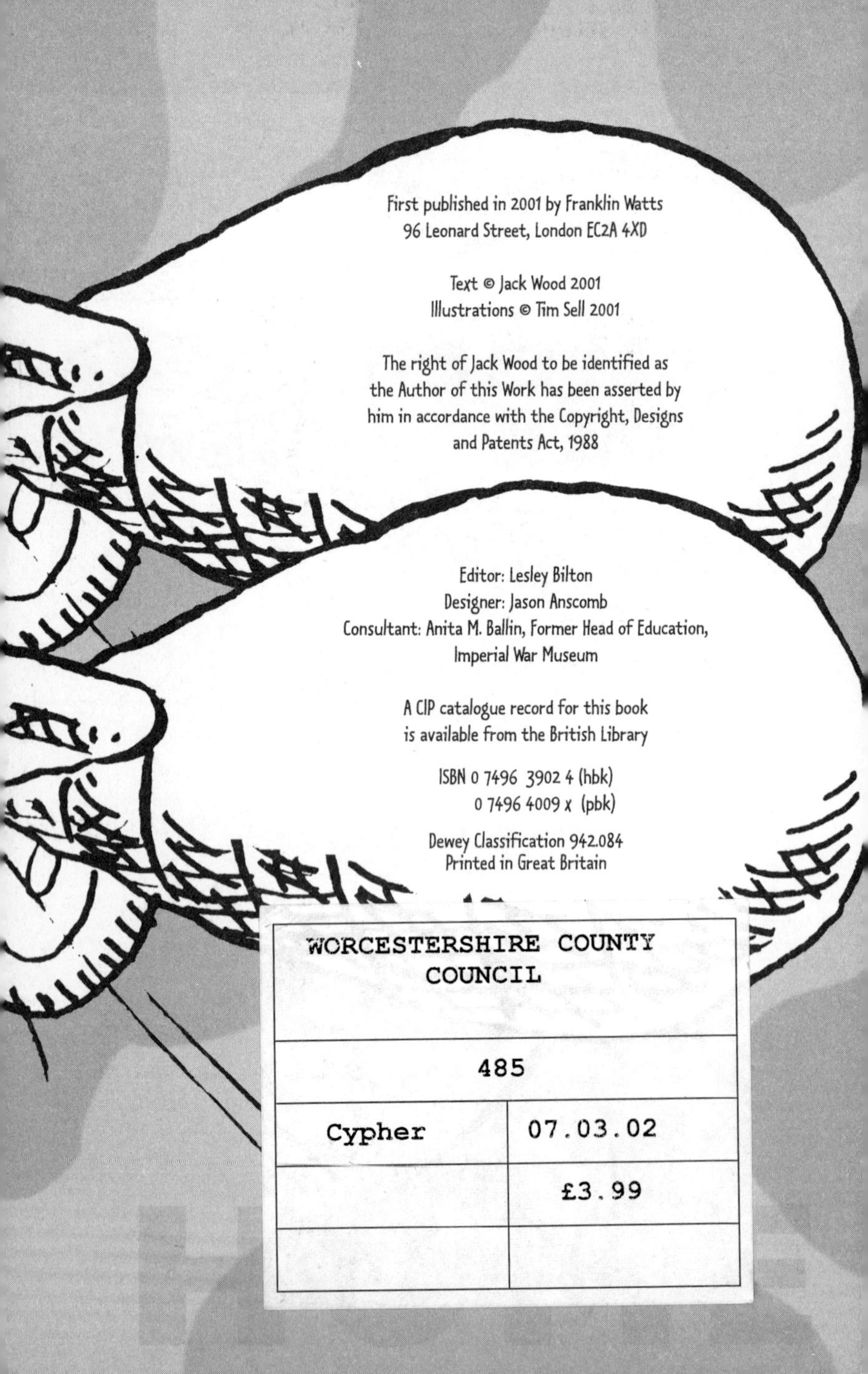

First published in 2001 by Franklin Watts
96 Leonard Street, London EC2A 4XD

Editor: Lesley Bilton
Designer: Jason Anscomb
Consultant: Anita M. Ballin, Former Head of Education, Imperial War Museum

A CIP catalogue record for this book is available from the British Library

ISBN 0 7496 3902 4 (hbk)
0 7496 4009 x (pbk)

Dewey Classification 942.084
Printed in Great Britain

HOME FRONT

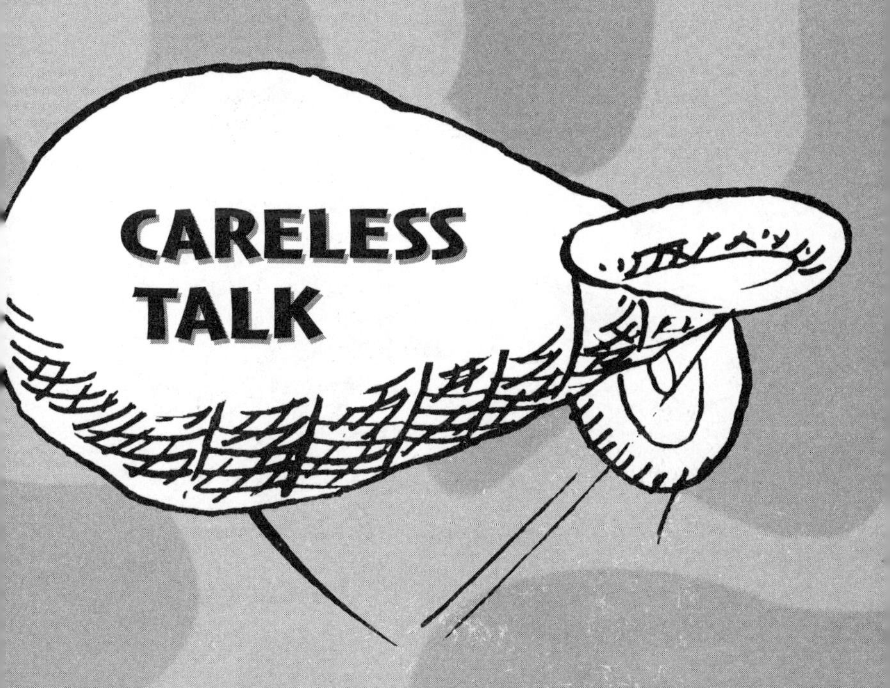

CARELESS TALK

by Jack Wood

Illustrations by Tim Sell

TALES OF THE SECOND WORLD WAR

LOOK OUT
THERE'S A SPY ABOUT
NUTS TO HITLER!

Chapter 1

Signs of the Times

"Well, what do you think?" Heather Pitt stood back and admired her drawing. "It's good, isn't it?"

Her brother Roy stopped scrabbling in the wreckage of the bombed-out house in Balaclava Terrace. He was collecting wood for the tree house he was building in the park. "It's not bad," he said, looking up.

As he was studying her charcoal sketch, Heather turned her attention to a poster on the wall. With an artistic flourish, she added a small black moustache to the man's face.

"I don't think *that* looks right," said Roy. "Hitler doesn't wear a raincoat like that."

"Not even in the rain?"

Roy took the charcoal from Heather's hand and advanced on the poster. "Perhaps if you added a . . ."

His hand had almost reached the poster when he was halted by a loud shout. "Stop defacing Government property this instant!"

A meaty hand closed on Roy's arm and spun him round. He found himself staring into an angry red face. It was Mr Marsh, their local Air-Raid Precautions Warden. He was

breathing heavily and, in the hand which wasn't clutching Roy, he brandished a signpost.

Behind him a smaller man, also wearing a warden's uniform, staggered under the weight of another signpost.

And behind him was a fat spotty boy carrying yet another signpost.

"It's Hubert," shouted Heather. "Hey Hubert! What are you doing?"

Hubert Moon, who lived next door to the Pitts in Balaclava Terrace, dropped the sign (labelled 'Fishmarket') on his foot.

"Owwee!" He hopped up and down, his pasty face contorted with pain.

The large warden dropped Roy's arm and turned on Hubert. "Be quiet, stupid boy, and pick up that sign immediately. Show some respect for Government property!"

"It's too heavy for me. I shouldn't be carrying it. I'm delicate. My Ma wouldn't like it," whined Hubert. But he stopped hopping and picked up the sign.

"Why are you taking away the street signs, Warden Marsh?" Roy asked.

"Quiet!" The warden shot a quick glance over his shoulder. "There are spies all around.

We're on important business. Everything possible must be done to hinder the enemy. No suspicious characters must be given information which might assist them in their activities. You see," he tapped his nose, "when those German spies are parachuted down, they won't know where to go because there won't be any street signs. So they'll have to ask the way. Then we'll arrest them."

"But what about strangers who aren't spies?" Roy was puzzled. "How will they know where to go?"

"Don't ask silly questions. Yes," Warden Marsh nodded, "when those German parachutists land – very probably disguised as nuns and possibly accompanied by highly-trained dogs – they'll be lost." *

**See other ways of confusing spies on page 60.*

“Why would they be dressed as nuns?” asked Heather.

“I can’t say any more. Careless Talk Costs Lives.* We Air-Raid Precautions Wardens know about these things. We’ve been specially trained. And it’s your duty to look out for spies.” He swelled with importance and

**Find out more about Careless Talk on page 61.*

pointed to the defaced poster. “And remember, walls have ears.” He clicked his fingers. “Come along, Bagshott. Shake a leg, young Moon.”

Shouldering his signpost, he lumbered off, followed by his two helpers. The procession wound its way round the corner leaving Roy and Heather gazing at the poster.

“Well, there’s not many people round here wear bowler hats and carry briefcases,” said Roy. “I’ve never seen anyone dressed like that.”

“I have,” said Heather. “He’s just moved into our street.”

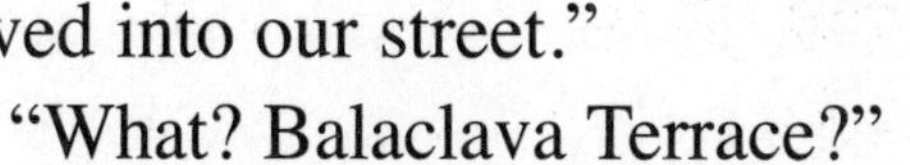

“What? Balaclava Terrace?”

“Yep. Number 42. Only two doors down – the other side of Mrs Moan.” (Hubert’s Ma, Mrs Moon, was known as Mrs Moan because

she never stopped moaning.) "He's got a wife. I saw them move in last week. A horse and cart arrived with a few bits of furniture. I asked if I could help, but the man just gave me a funny look and shook his head."

"I don't believe he looked just like that," Roy nodded at the poster.

"He did. Exactly the same. I'll show you this afternoon," Heather said, turning away and heading for home.

Chapter 2

A Suspicious Person

But that afternoon Ma took them all shopping. Or rather took them all queueing. Roy and Heather were used to it. Ever since the war started, it had been the same. If you wanted anything – you queued.

And queued.

Ma and Heather joined the queue outside Mr Trotter's butcher's shop.

Joanie stood over the road in the fishmonger's queue.

Dad tagged onto the end of the queue outside the tobacconists.

And Lenny had heard a rumour that some razor blades might be arriving at the chemists. So Roy was sent there to queue.

Lenny himself was queueing for batteries.

Then, when the entire Pitt family (except for Gran), was standing in queues, it started to rain.

Heather tried to protect herself from the downpour.

"Put that newspaper down," said Ma, smacking Heather with the food ration book. "We'll need it to wrap up the meat. *If* there's any left by the time it's our turn to be served."

"But I'm getting wet."

"So what? Girls are easy to dry. Wrapping paper's scarce."

Heather obeyed miserably, shoving the precious newspaper up her jumper.

"Look!" Roy ran up to them, waving a bar of soap. "No razor blades, but I did get this!"

Ma grabbed the soap eagerly. "*Soap*," she said in a gloating voice. "It's been ages since we had any soap." She turned to her neighbours in the queue. "Here, Madge, Irene, see what our Roy's got." The women on either side of Ma looked at the soap with envy and passed it from hand to hand.

"Look, that's him," hissed Heather, nudging Roy in the ribs. "That's the man who's moved into Number 42."

Roy looked up. A small man wearing a raincoat was striding down the street. A lowered umbrella covered his face.

Roy gave the man a penetrating stare, and checked his appearance against the poster.

Bowler hat.

Yes.

Raincoat.

Yes.

Briefcase.

Yes.

Umbrella.

Yes.

Everything matched! There could be no doubt about it – the man was a spy!

The spy scuttled past, ignoring the queue, but Ma had already spotted him.

"Good afternoon," she said politely. "Nice weather for ducks."

The man gave Ma a popeyed stare, and made a strangled sort of noise at the back of his throat. Then he pulled a huge hanky out of his pocket, and pretended to sneeze. Keeping the hanky over his face, he lowered his umbrella and charged off down the road.

"How rude," sniffed Ma.

"Who is he, Ma?" asked Heather.

"I don't know his name, but he's just moved into Number 42. I think he's got a wife. Queenie Moan saw the curtains twitch as he left the house yesterday morning."

(Mrs Moan didn't miss much.)

They watched the man as he disappeared down the road and round the corner.

Heather tugged Roy's sleeve. "Let's follow."

"And where do you think you're going, madam?" Ma tightened her grip on Heather, as muttering spread through the butcher's queue.

The woman in front of Ma turned to her. "He's got some sausages," she hissed.

The listening women shivered with excitement.

"Leave it to me. I'll follow him," whispered Roy to Heather.

"He's got some chops!" quavered a voice at the front of the queue.

Excitement became intense. The waiting women surged forward, clutching their baskets and wrapping paper.

"Roy," Ma grabbed his arm, "go and tell our Joanie to get herself here – double-quick! You take her place in the fish queue."

"But Ma, I want to –"

"Get Joanie," said Ma in her fiercest voice. "Porky Trotter is sweet on her. If there are

chops under his counter, then our Joanie's the one to get them."

Roy threw a despairing look down the street. It was no good – there was no sign of the little man. With a sigh, he trotted down the road towards the fishmonger's queue.

Fancy letting a spy escape for the sake of a few mouldy old chops!

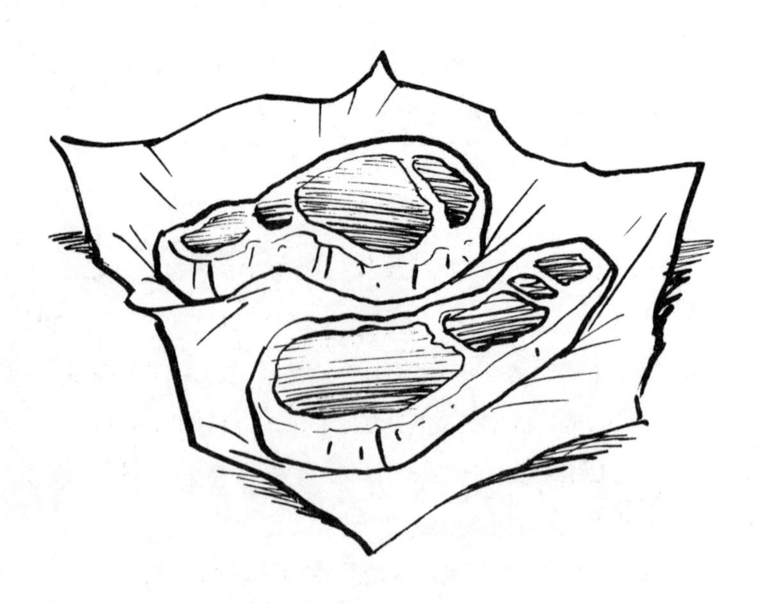

Chapter 3

Censored!

As it turned out, they didn't get any chops. They'd run out before Joanie reached the front of the queue. But Dad dug up some potatoes, and Ma found a bit of bacon left over from last week's ration. Bacon and chips! Now if Gran's hens had laid some eggs . . .

They hadn't, and Gran was very cross about it. "My hens have been put off laying by all the noise. That man who's just moved into Number 42 is making a racket in his garden. It shouldn't be allowed. I think he's building a shed for his pigeons."

"Pigeons?" echoed Roy, giving Heather a meaningful look. "Homing pigeons? The type that carry messages tied to their legs?"

"I don't know what sort of birds they are," snorted Gran. "They can be ostriches for all I care, provided they don't disturb my hens. Only one measly egg in the last three days!" Gran turned and stomped towards the kitchen. "Oh, and talking of messages," she called over her shoulder, "there's a letter for you, Joanie. I put it under the wireless."

Joanie ran across the room and lifted up the wireless. "It must be from my Stan," she said, picking up the envelope and tearing it open. "He said he'd write to me as soon as he knew where he was posted."

It didn't take her long to read the letter. "He doesn't say very much," she said, tossing it down on the table.

The Pitts crowded round and read Joanie's letter in silence. It didn't take them long to read either, because most of the words had been crossed out with a thick black pen.

Dear Joanie,
I can't say where we are but the weather is very ███ and the scenery is ███ ███ ███.
It isn't half ███!
We took ███ days to get here. First we went in a ███ ███ and then they transferred us to a ███.
For dinner we had ███ and chips.
Must go now and polish my ███.
Love Stan
xxx.

"Well," said Ma. "It's not exactly full of news."

Dad sighed. "Well, it wouldn't be, would it. It's been censored." *

"What's that mean?" asked Heather.

**Find out about censorship on page 61*

"It means some officer has been through Stan's letter and crossed out all the secret bits," explained Dad.

"Oh."

There was a silence while they all thought about this.

"But *why* can't Stan tell me where he is?" wondered Joanie as she folded the letter and put it back in the envelope.

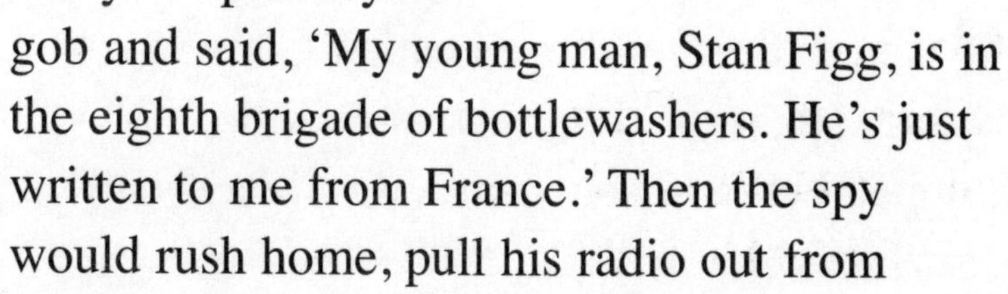

"In case you tell anyone," said Dad, taking the envelope. "You see, suppose you were queueing outside Porky Trotter's for sausages and a spy was standing behind you, and you opened your gob and said, 'My young man, Stan Figg, is in the eighth brigade of bottlewashers. He's just written to me from France.' Then the spy would rush home, pull his radio out from

under the bed, get through to Germany and tell Hitler that Stan was in France."

"How would that help Hitler?"

"You never know," said Dad mysteriously.

"But why can't Stan tell us what he had to eat?" asked Heather.

"Wee-eelll," Dad thought hard. "Suppose it was German sausage. Then we'd know –"

"How's German sausage different from ordinary sausage?" asked Roy.

"Bigger and smellier, and don't interrupt your elders. As I was saying," continued Dad, "if Stan told us he'd been eating German sausage, then we'd know that he'd been dropped behind enemy lines. Or if he'd had curry, we'd know he was in India."

"India! What would my Stan be doing in India?" Joanie wailed. "Stan can't stand the heat. He comes out in a prickly rash. Why have they sent him to India?"

"I didn't say they had," said Dad getting flustered. "Anyway, that's what censorship is. I'm going to the Fishgutters'. Coming, Lenny?"

"You are *not* going to the pub," said Ma folding her arms.

"Sorry. Duty calls," said Dad. "We're looking for spies."

"Oh really?" Ma moved in front of the door. "In the Fishgutters' Arms?"

"Yes," said Lenny. "Didn't you hear? They caught a spy in the next town. He went into a pub at nine in the morning and asked for a glass of sherry."

"He'd been badly trained, you see," Dad dropped his voice. "They didn't tell him at the

German spy school that pubs in England don't serve drinks in the morning."

Roy's eyes went round.

"So," continued Lenny, "Dad's guarding the public bar of the Fishgutters' and I'm on duty in the snug." Lenny flexed his muscles. "I'll soon fix any German spy asking for a drink outside of opening hours." He strode out of the room closely followed by Dad.

Roy and Heather scuttled after them.

"And where do you two think you're going?" Ma snapped.

"We're just going out to play. The rain's stopped now."

"You said we could."

"Not until you've helped me peel some potatoes," said Ma. "We need lots of chips tonight to go with that bacon."

Chapter 4

Keeping Watch

As soon as they had finished helping Ma, Roy and Heather escaped out of the front door. And the first thing they saw, sitting on a wall of the bombed-out house opposite, was Hubert Moon. His cheeks were bulging and he made loud sucking noises.

"What are you doing here, Hubert?"

"Can't you find any signposts to carry?"

Hubert fished a chunk of treacle toffee out of his mouth and looked at it thoughtfully. "No, they've finished with them. They took them all to a big shed behind the Town Hall and locked them up. They took down the sign showing the name of the railway station last. I watched 'em. Then there was nothing left to watch because they'd taken everything. So I came back here."

"Have you seen a man come out of Number 42?"

"What's he look like?"

"He wears a raincoat and a bowler hat and carries a briefcase," explained Roy. "Have you seen him?"

Hubert licked his toffee thoughtfully. "I might have. Why do you want to know?"

"We think he's a spy."

"Huh!" Hubert wrapped a hanky round his toffee and shoved it in his pocket. "It doesn't look like a spy's house."

It didn't. Number 42 Balaclava Terrace was boringly tidy and respectable. In fact it was much more respectable than the Pitts' house. Clean net curtains guarded the gleaming windows and the freshly polished front door step shone.

Roy wasn't discouraged. "Gran says he keeps pigeons.

They could be used to send messages.* What's the building round the back?"

"I don't know. I haven't looked. It's rude to stare into other people's gardens."

"You'll be sorry if he is a spy."

"All right. We'll go into my garden and you can check it out."

The three of them slunk down the alley which separated their two houses, and slipped through the gate into Hubert's back garden. The shared fence between the Moons' garden

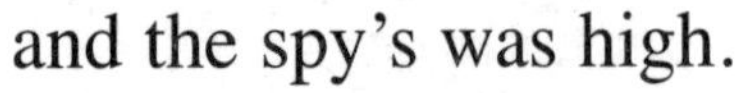

and the spy's was high.

"You're smallest, Heather," said Roy, bending down. She scrambled up on his shoulders and peered over the fence.

"Well, what can you see?"

"There's some washing pegged out on the line."

**Pigeons were useful in wartime – see page 63.*

"So what?" Hubert was unimpressed.

"It's been raining all afternoon. Why hasn't she brought the clothes in?"

Silence. None of them could think of a good answer to this question.

"There's an awful lot of handkerchiefs."

"That doesn't mean anything, stupid."

"They might be pegged out in a pattern," grunted Roy. His shoulders were hurting. "It could be a signal to low-flying German planes, telling them where to drop their bombs."

"What? You mean nine hankies, three pairs of knickers and a nightie are a message?" scoffed Heather.

"I can't hold you up any more. You're too heavy." With a groan Roy collapsed onto the ground, and brought Heather tumbling down beside him.

Hubert lowered himself on to a sandbag, took out his hanky and unwrapped his toffee slowly. "The washing could be a code," he said, "telling the Germans that nine battleships and three destroyers are leaving the harbour tonight."

Roy's jaw dropped.

So did Heather's.

Roy was the first to find his voice. "Why Hubert, that's clever!"

"I know." Hubert contemplated his toffee with satisfaction. "I am."

"Did you see anything else suspicious, Heather? What about the pigeons? Were there any –"

Roy broke off and cocked his head. A woman's voice floated through the air. It came from inside the spy's house. "Bye bye, dear. Remember your instructions, and keep well muffled up."

They looked at each other.

"She doesn't sound German," said Heather. "I wonder what instructions she's talking about?"

"She's warning him to keep his face masked in case people recognise that he's a spy."

Hubert was getting positively masterly.

They heard a door slam.

"Come on. That sounded like the front door shutting. He's leaving the house. Let's follow and see what he's up to," said Roy, picking himself up from the ground. "Hurry up or we'll lose him."

Heather was the first to scramble to her feet and rush out of the garden. Hubert and Roy were close behind. With a mad dash the three of them sprinted down the alley and into Balaclava Terrace.

Chapter 5

The Chase

They were just in time to see the little man walking briskly down the street.

"He's still wearing that raincoat."

"And he's carrying a bag thing."

"It's a briefcase."

"What's that?"

"It's for carrying important papers in," said Hubert. "Secrets and plans and stuff. I saw a film once, and there was this man who was a spy, only he wasn't a German spy, he was an English spy, but he had a false moustache to make himself look foreign. Well, he had a briefcase and he –"

"Quick, he's turning down Alma Road."

They ran to the end of Balaclava Terrace and reached the corner in time to see the spy turn into Inkerman Street.

They stopped talking and followed him for about ten minutes. At one point they almost bumped into him. He'd come to a halt by the entrance to Parsons Park and was looking puzzled. There was a gap where the old signpost used to be.

"He doesn't know where he's going," said Heather.

"That's one of the signposts that I helped remove this morning," said Hubert importantly.

"Quick. He's off again."

They stalked him more cautiously down several streets and alleys. "He's going to the docks," said Heather.

She was right. The South Dock was the spy's destination. He walked almost up to the edge of the quay and sat down on a bench. Then he opened his mouth and took several deep breaths. When he'd finished that he rummaged in his pocket and brought out a handkerchief.

They watched in suspense.

"He's blowing his nose."

"Probably signalling to a submarine."

"How would a submarine hear that?"

"He's getting something out of his bag."

The spy produced a notebook and a pencil from the briefcase.

"He's drawing the boats. He's showing the location of things of military importance."

"What's important about Salty Shaw's old fishing boat?"

"You never know."

"Look, he's getting something else out."

The spy was lifting a brown paper bag from his case. He placed it on the bench. Then spreading the hanky across his knee, he lifted the bag on it, and took out a large sandwich.

They watched as he ate it, nibbling daintily and chewing each mouthful slowly. Several times he stopped to blow his nose. Then he looked round to the left, and the right. Then flung down the crust. A crowd of birds flew down and pecked at his feet.

"He's throwing bread for the birds. They could have just arrived from Germany with messages tied to their legs."

"What do we do? We still haven't got definite proof that he's a spy." Roy chewed his thumb. "How can we find out?"

"I saw a film once," squeaked Hubert,

"and someone said something in German to someone they thought was a spy, and the person they thought was a spy answered in German without thinking. So then they *knew* he was a spy."

Roy considered the idea. “But we don’t know any German.”

“Try shouting ‘*Achtung*!’”

“What’s that mean?”

“I don’t know, but the Germans are always saying it in films.”

“Right. Go on then.”

“Not me,” Hubert shook his head. “My Ma wouldn’t want me to. I’m delicate.”

“You’re useless.” Roy squared his shoulders and advanced on the spy who’d started on a second sandwich. Taking a deep breath Roy leaped forward and shouted in the spy’s left ear, “***Achtung***!”

As an experiment it was a failure. The man in the raincoat didn't answer in German. Or in English. He just swung round with an alarmed look on his face, made a strangled growling noise deep in his throat, dropped his sandwich and rushed off like the wind.

They watched in silence as he sprinted down the quayside and round the nearest corner.

"He hasn't taken his briefcase. Let's get it," said Heather. "He might have left his notebook in it."

"It might be booby-trapped." Hubert clutched her arm. "I think we should follow him and see where he goes."

Roy dithered. He was torn between the bag and the vanishing spy.

"You follow him, Heather. Here," he dug in his pocket for the piece of charcoal and thrust it in her hand. "Draw arrows on the pavement and we'll come after you. Stick with him."

Heather looked unhappy. "I'll miss tea. It's bacon."

"Never mind bacon. Think of your country. Scoot."

She scooted.

Roy advanced on the briefcase slowly.

Hubert retreated behind a conveniently placed pile of sandbags. "It might have a secret compartment that's wired with a bomb. And if you don't open it the right way, it'll blow you up. I saw this film once and –"

Roy blocked his ears to Hubert's babbling and reached for the briefcase gingerly. He thought of the possible bomb. Then he remembered telling Heather to think of her country. So he closed his eyes and thought of England. Then he opened the case.

It was empty. Rats! The spy must have pushed the notebook into his pocket.

"He'd hardly started his second sandwich." Hubert looked at the food hungrily. "I wonder what's in it." He lifted the top piece of bread and sniffed at the filling. "Pooh! What smelly sausage!"

Roy snatched the slice of meat out of the sandwich. It was very large and extremely smelly. "It must be *German* sausage."

Roy and Hubert's eyes met. What more proof could be needed? "He *is* a spy!" said Hubert with awe. "We'd better tell somebody."

"Who?"

"Someone in authority. What about Warden Marsh?"

"No fear. We'll ask Dad and Lenny."

"Where are they?"

"In the Fishgutters' watching for spies. Let's go!"

Chapter 6

Hubert the Hero

But Lenny wasn't in the Fishgutters' Arms. He was *outside*, leaning against the doorway, and feeling rather unwell. Checking for spies was a long job, and he'd had a bit too much to drink. Fortunately for the sake of Britain's security, Dad was still inside the pub, conscientiously scrutinising the other drinkers while downing pints of beer.

The spy catchers gathered round Lenny.

"Washing . . ."

"Pigeons . . ."

"Docks . . ."

"German sausage . . ."

"Hold your horses!" said Lenny, shaking his head in an effort to clear it. "I can't take this all in." He staggered to the door of the pub and croaked, "Dad, can you come out here?"

Several minutes passed before Dad lounged out into the street. He wasn't very pleased. "What do you think you're doing?

Don't you know better than to interrupt a man when he's doing his duty?" He looked down and noticed the children for the first time. "And what are you lot doing here? You'll catch it from your Ma, Hubert Moon, loitering outside the pub." Dad laughed loudly and wiped his mouth with his hand.

"No, listen. It's serious," Roy pulled his sleeve and began to talk urgently.

Dad heard the story in silence, taking only occasional slurps of beer to help his thought processes.

"Well I must say, it does sound a bit odd. And we don't know much about the chap. Perhaps we'd better look into it, eh Lenny?"

"I suppose we ought to check it out. Where did the blighter go?"

"Heather's following him. She's leaving a trail."

It wasn't a difficult track to follow. The charcoal arrows led straight from the

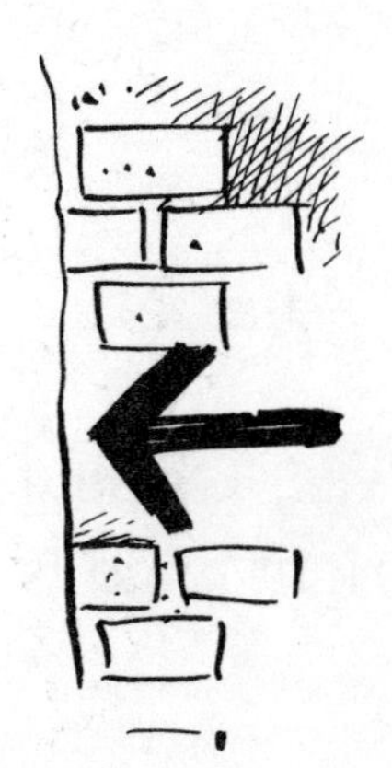

docks to Balaclava Terrace. Heather was lurking behind a wall in the bombed-out house opposite.

"He just ran all the way back to his house and slammed the door behind him. Then," she lowered her voice, "your Ma came out of your house, Hubert. And she knocked on his door. And it opened and she went in. That was ages ago and she hasn't come out."

Hubert looked worried. "He could have taken her prisoner – be holding her as a hostage." His lower lip began to tremble. "If anything happens to Ma, who's going to look after me? Who's going to do the cooking?"

"Oh shut up," said Dad. "No-one in their right mind is going to hold your Ma hostage.

She'd drive 'em mad. Talk the hind leg off a donkey would your Ma. Still, I suppose we ought to find out if anything's happened to her. We'd better make a plan of action. Any ideas, Lenny?"

Lenny thought hard. "I think a two-pronged offensive will be best," he said eventually. "We'll attack from the rear. Dad and I will go through the garden and effect an entry through the back door, while you, Hubert, distract this chap's attention by knocking on the front door."

"Me?" squeaked Hubert. "But he might have a gun!"

"Yes, you," said Dad. "It's only natural for you to go looking for your Ma. If any of us knocked on the door, it could rouse his suspicions."

Hubert's legs shook. "But he might take me prisoner as well. And I'm delicate. Can't Roy go?"

"No, I can't," said Roy. "After all, it's *your* Ma."

"Pretend it's a film, and you're the star," suggested Heather.

Hubert carried on shaking, but a gleam of interest appeared in his piggy eyes. "I'm the star?" he murmured.

"Yes," said Heather, warming to her subject. "Nobody else dares to make a move, but you won't let anything stand in your way. You burst into the house, careless of any danger, overpower the spy, grab his gun, and save your Ma. Then you're summoned to London and the grateful Government gives you a medal for heroism."

Hubert's eyes took on a faraway look. "I'm the star," he repeated.

"Yes. And your name will be in big letters across the top of all the posters," said Heather firmly.

"All right. I'll do it!"

"Good, let's get cracking," commanded Dad. "Lenny and I will go down the alley to the garden. Then you, Hubert, count to twenty after we've gone and then knock on the front door."

Hubert wiped his forehead. "I don't feel very well," he gulped. "I'm not sure I want to be a star after all." But he did take a step in the direction of the door.

They were never to know whether Hubert's courage would have carried him through or not, because at that moment the door of Number 42 opened, and out popped Mrs Moon.

Hubert rushed across the road and flung his arms around her. "Are you all right, Ma? What's for tea?"

Chapter 7

The Last of the Spy

"Why shouldn't I be all right?" Mrs Moon patted Hubert on the head. "I've just had ever such a nice chat with Mrs Harbottle and her poor husband. She's such a nice woman. And he's ever such a nice man too. It's such a shame. What a terrible time that poor couple have had. Yes," she repeated with relish, "a terrible time."

"Oh, what happened to them?"

"Well, they were bombed, poor things. A bomb fell through their roof and landed on the bed. But it was a delayed action bomb, so they

got out of the house just before it blew up. All he saved was his working suit and his briefcase, while poor Mrs Harbottle only managed to grab a large sausage – a Christmas present from her sister who married a Frenchman – as she ran through the kitchen."

"Why take a sausage?" asked Heather.

Mrs Moon forged on with her story, ignoring her. "So then they were put into temporary accommodation, and it was so damp they both got influenza and then his turned to terrible tonsillitis. So they took him into hospital last week and whipped out his tonsils. Mrs Harbottle says that the back of his throat's red raw. The doctor's told him not to talk for a month – otherwise he can't speak for the consequences. And the handkerchiefs the poor man goes through!* Such a trial in a time of clothes rationing. Mrs Harbottle was telling me that she has to cut up old bed sheets and hem them."

"But why does he go hanging round the docks if he's ill?" Roy wasn't going to give up his spy without a fight.

"Sea air is good for him and he's been told to get lungfuls of it every day. He's very delicate. Like my Hubert." Mrs Moon stroked her son's curls and a cloud of dandruff floated on to his shoulders. "Come on, lambkin, time for tea. I've got a nice bit of bacon."

**People were told to use hankies – see page 63.*

Hubert smirked as his Ma led him into the house.

Dad glared at Roy. “What a waste of time! Back to the Fishgutters’, Lenny! God knows how many spies have got away while we’ve been on this wild goose chase.” He sloped off up the road, closely followed by Lenny.

It was getting dark. Roy and Heather looked at each other. They were the only people left in the street.

“Well, he jolly well looked exactly like that spy poster,” complained Roy. “They shouldn’t go round putting up misleading posters.” He kicked a bit of shrapnel with his foot. “What a rotten day!”

“Oh, I don’t know,” said Heather sniffing. A tasty smell was wafting from the open window of their house. “We’ve got bacon for tea, too.”

“True,” said Roy brightening up.

“*And* it looks like Dad and Lenny won’t be there for their share.”

Roy grinned and followed his sister into the house.

46

NOTES

Signposts and Church Bells

In 1940, there was a real danger that the German army would invade Britain. So all signposts were taken down, making it hard for the enemy to find their way around. Railway station signs were also removed – you had to ask people where you were. Churches were forbidden to ring their bells, except as a signal that the Germans had arrived.

Careless Talk

It was thought that German spies would pick up useful information by listening to ordinary people's conversations. So members of the public were urged not to talk about anything that could help the enemy. The Government produced a series of posters warning people not to discuss the war in public in case German agents heard them.

Censorship

When soldiers were sent abroad, their only contact with home was by post. The letters they wrote were censored. They were read by an officer to make sure that they didn't give away any secrets or information which would be useful to the enemy.

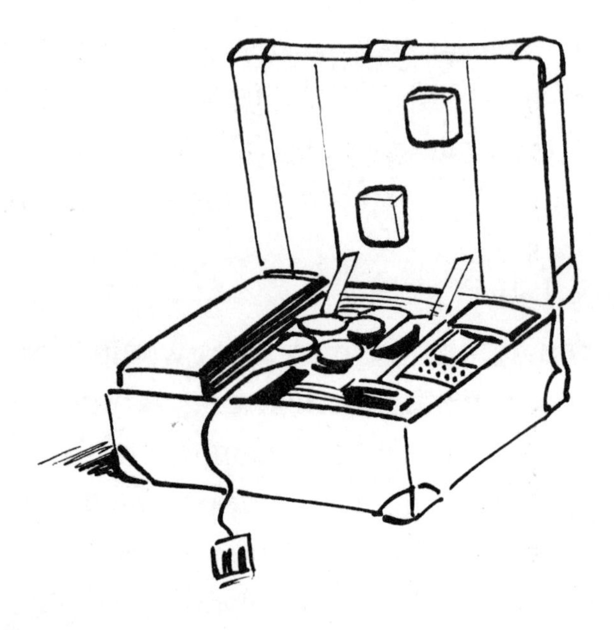

Spies

The Government warned that enemy spies could be living undercover and sending messages to Germany by wireless. The public were told to report anyone behaving suspiciously. Unfortunate people with foreign-sounding names were treated with special caution. Everyone was issued with an identity card to prove who they were. Anyone in authority could ask you to produce your card.

Pigeons

Throughout history pigeons have been used to carry messages. In 1937, the National Pigeon Service was formed and 200,000 birds were given to the defence forces for the purposes of sending messages.

Keeping Healthy

If people were to work effectively in wartime and endure the air raids and food shortages, they had to be fit. The Government was particularly concerned about the spread of germs. They published a booklet called *How to Keep Well in Wartime* which told everyone to use their handkerchiefs, because coughs and sneezes spread diseases.

The Pitt Family

Find out more about how the Pitts survived the Second World War.

Digging for Victory 0 7496 3866 4 (Hbk) 0 7496 3960 1 (Pbk)

Spam! Whale meat! Boiled nettles! More Spam! The Pitts have had enough of food rationing. Then Lenny finds a crate of tinned fruit . . .

Make Do and Mend 0 7496 3903 2 (Hbk) 0 7496 4010 3 (Pbk)

The Pitts are fed up with clothes rationing. They've nothing left to wear. Then Roy obtains a parachute, and the trouble begins . . .

Put That Light Out! 0 7496 3867 2 (Hbk) 0 7496 3961 X (Pbk)

Dad's fallen down a bomb crater! Lenny's walked into a lamp post! The Pitt family is having trouble in the blackout. Then the air-raid siren goes off . . .